A Dog Named HAKU

A Holiday Story from NEPAL

Margarita Engle with Amish Karanjit and Nicole Karanjit

Illustrated by Ruth Jeyaveeran

M Millbrook Press/Minneapolis

For my grandchildren
—M.E.

For our daughter, Maya, and for our parents and siblings
—A.K. and N.K.

For all the children and animals affected by earthquakes
and hurricanes around the world
—R.J.

A Note to Readers
This story describes only one of many Hindu traditions from a five-day festival
variously known in Nepal as Swanti, Tihar, or Deepawali. In India, the festival
is often called Diwali or Deepavali. Houses and streets are lit up at night,
animals are honored, and people make beautiful patterns on floors using
colored rice, flour, sand, or flower petals. The date of the festival varies each
year depending on phases of the moon, but it always follows another
long festival called Dashain.

Grateful acknowledgment to Uma Krishnaswami
and Padma Venkatraman and her daughter
Karuna for reviewing the text and illustrations
and offering their feedback.

E
461-1714

Alu and Bhalu were brothers
who knew that the whole beautiful city
of Kathmandu
was ready to celebrate
its courageous dogs.

An earthquake had struck
in the spring,
and people were buried
under sliding rocks
and piles of broken
bricks.

Search and rescue dogs
sniffed the rubble
of tumbled buildings
and showed men and women
where to dig
to save those
who had been trapped.

Now, many months later,
Bhalu and Alu roamed
through the ruins of ancient temples

looking for a stray dog—a *kukur*—
to honor with food
and gratitude.

On other festival days,
people would feed crows or ravens,
decorate cars and cows,
or give gifts to brothers and sisters,

but today was the
time to honor
every kukur.

Alu and Bhalu searched and searched,
but they could not find even one dog to feed.

Many other children were already
feeding treats to all sorts of dogs
while Bhalu and Alu wandered
among twirling kites,
spinning Ferris wheels,
and towering bamboo swings

called *pings*, ridden by boys and girls
who shrieked as they soared,
                                        flying
                                                so high!

By nighttime, the sky
sparkled with fireworks,
and families chased away the darkness
by lighting lanterns on doorsteps,
rooftops,
and windowsills . . .

but Alu and Bhalu still had not found
a hungry kukur, so they searched
one more time, because they remembered
how rescue dogs kept searching
for them.

At home, the boys' mother
prepared a feast flavored with
red, yellow, and orange spices.

The boys' father wondered
where his young sons might be, but Dalli—
the clever little sister of two mischievous brothers—
smiled because secretly, she knew
what they must be doing.

Finally, on a dark corner
without any lanterns
or fireworks,
Bhalu and Alu
found a puppy
wandering

homeless,
        motherless,
            lonely.

The dog's soft fur was black,
so the boys decided to call her Haku.

Alu and Bhalu took turns carrying
poor Haku to their house,
at last arriving,

trying not to scatter
the rice flour
arranged in dazzling patterns
on the living room floor.

The boys knew their parents must be worried
because they'd been gone so long,
but they needed more treats for Haku.

So they snuck into the kitchen,
and Alu quietly grabbed a plate of dumplings
and Bhalu silently snatched a dish of sweets
and then the naughty brothers tiptoed

all the way
    up,
        up,
           up
              to the lantern-lit rooftop.

Just then a crowd of grown-ups
charged up the stairs—
parents, grannies, aunties, and uncles—

all wondering why they heard
barks, yips, yaps,
and giggles.

Soon everyone was sitting
in a circle, beneath dazzling fireworks
brilliant stars, and a glowing moon
while Dalli
painted a red *tika*
on Haku's forehead,

and Alu and Bhalu
draped garlands
of orange flowers
around the puppy's neck.

Everyone agreed that
on the festival's special brother-sister
gift-giving day, all three children

should generously give one another
one lonely puppy
who needed
a home.

All the grown-ups smiled
as they bowed their heads
to give thanks.
Namaste.

Glossary of Nepali Words

Alu (ah-loo): potato. In this story, it is an affectionate nickname.

Bhalu (bah-loo): bear. In this story, it is an affectionate nickname.

Dalli (dah-lee): round-faced. In this story, it is an affectionate nickname.

haku (ha-koo): black. In this story, it is an affectionate nickname.

Kathmandu (cat-mahn-doo): the capital city of Nepal

kukur (kuh-kuhr): dog

namaste (nah-muh-stay): a traditional greeting and way of saying thank you, accompanied by a bowed head with hands in a position of prayer

Nepal (nay-pahl): a small Asian country located on the northeast border of India and south of China

ping (ping): twenty-foot-tall bamboo swing

tika (tee-kuh): a ceremonial red dot painted on the forehead to show respect

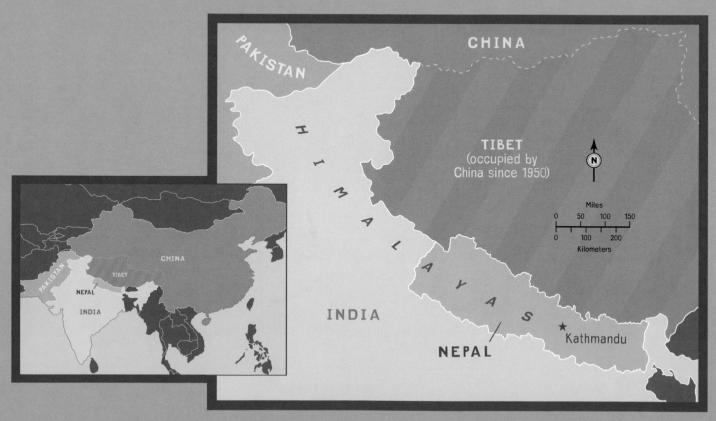

Learn More about Nepal

Dinerstein, Eric. *What Elephants Know*. New York: Disney-Hyperion, 2016.

Heine, Theresa. *Chandra's Magic Light: A Story in Nepal*. Cambridge, MA: Barefoot Books, 2014.

King, Dedie. *I See the Sun in Nepal*. Hardwick, MA: Satya House, 2014.

Young, Ed. *I, Doko: The Tale of a Basket*. New York: Philomel Books, 2004.

Zuchora-Walske, Christine. *Nepal in Pictures*. Minneapolis: Twenty-First Century Books, 2009.

Suggested Activities

Draw pictures of ping swings and other festival activities.

Decorate your room at home or your school classroom with garlands of real blossoms or paper flowers.

Decorate a floor with colorful paper designs. To draw shapes like those used in the story, see http://coloringmandalas.blogspot.com/p/overview.html. For more complex shapes, see http://www.4kraftykidz.com/AdultColoring_MANDALAS.html.

Find a Nepali-English dictionary online, and learn how to write *kukur* in the alphabet.

Raise funds for an international charity that helps people affected by natural disasters.

Raise funds for a no-kill animal shelter that helps take care of homeless dogs in your own neighborhood.

Invite a local search and rescue dog trainer to talk to your class at school.

Amish's uncle, Shyam Karanjit, shared this photo of his dog Zhera in Kathmandu in October 2017.

Millbrook Press
A division of Lerner Publishing Group, Inc.
241 First Avenue North
Minneapolis, MN 55401 USA

For reading levels and more information, look up this title at www.lernerbooks.com.

Designed by Danielle Carnito.
Main body text set in Imperfect OT 19/24. Typeface provided by T26.
The illustrations in this book were created with a combination of hand drawing and digital imagery.

Library of Congress Cataloging-in-Publication Data

Names: Engle, Margarita, author. | Karanjit, Amish, author. | Karanjit, Nicole, author. | Jeyaveeran, Ruth, illustrator.
Title: A dog named Haku : a holiday story from Nepal / by Margarita Engle with Amish Karanjit and Nicole Karanjit ; illustrated by Ruth Jeyaveeran.
Description: Minneapolis : Millbrook Press, [2018] | Summary: During a Hindu festival in Kathmandu, Nepal, brothers Alu and Bhalu search for a dog they can honor with food and gratitude. Includes glossary of Nepali words and suggested activities. | Includes bibliographical references.
Identifiers: LCCN 2017046990 (print) | LCCN 2017057742 (ebook) | ISBN 9781541524699 (eb pdf) | ISBN 9781512432053 (lb : alk. paper)
Subjects: | CYAC: Brothers—Fiction. | Dogs—Fiction. | Divali—Fiction. | Family life—Nepal—Fiction. | Nepal—Fiction.
Classification: LCC PZ7.E7158 (ebook) | LCC PZ7.E7158 Dog 2018 (print) | DDC [E]—dc23

LC record available at https://lccn.loc.gov/2017046990

Manufactured in the United States of America
1-41727-23521-2/8/2018